CO ANTRIM & CO LONDONDERRY

First published in Great Britain in 2010 by
Young Writers, Remus House, Coltsfoot Drive,
Peterborough, PE2 9JX
Tel (01733) 890066 Fax (01733) 313524
www.youngwriters.co.uk

SB ISBN 978-1-84924-919-5

Foreword

Since Young Writers was established in 1990, our aim has been to promote and encourage written creativity amongst children and young adults. By giving aspiring young authors the chance to be published, Young Writers effectively nurtures the creative talents of the next generation, allowing their confidence and writing ability to grow.

With our latest fun competition, *The Adventure Starts Here …* , secondary school children nationwide were given the tricky challenge of writing a story with a beginning, middle and an end in just fifty words.

The diverse and imaginative range of entries made the selection process a difficult but enjoyable task with stories chosen on the basis of style, expression, flair and technical skill. A fascinating glimpse into the imaginations of the future, we hope you will agree that this entertaining collection is one that will amuse and inspire the whole family.

Contents

St Columb's College, Derry

The Mini Sagas

The Swarm Of The Zombies

My friends and I were in class, when a bomb came through the window. It sprayed the teacher with green slime. In the hall, we met other teachers who had become zombies. A major battle took place. Many of my friends were killed, but Jack and I were born survivors.

Kyle Robert Doherty (11)
Campbell College, Belfast

Thump!

The car skidded off the road and crashed into the fence, but still continued! He reversed his badly damaged car back onto the road. Looking behind him, he saw nothing but another car about to smash into him! The passenger was leaning out of the car window, pointing a gun!

Chris Nesbitt (12)

Campbell College, Belfast

Christmas Dawn

Charlie crept out of bed and into his slippers
so silently, straight down the stairs and into the
kitchen. The carrots were gone, milk too! He
rushed to the lounge, but the stocking was empty.
Footsteps were coming ever closer … 'Santa?' he
whispered and, 'Ho! Ho! Ho!' came back …

Stewart Joseph Ian (11)
Campbell College, Belfast

The Forest

I was walking through the forest, *crunch, crunch, crunch,* on all the leaves and branches. I then heard this loud howl. I looked around, but no one was there, then it happened again. It started to chase me, but I don't know where it came from. Then it struck me …

Jacob McDowell (12)
Campbell College, Belfast

The Unexpected Attack

Bang! Aliens flood into our spaceship. *Zap!* My comrade gets shot and then collapses. People everywhere are getting annihilated. I want to save them, but I can't! Everything has suddenly gone black … my bones weaken, I have failed my team.

Game Over!

'Tom, come get your dinner!' called my mum.

Tom Robertson (11)

Campbell College, Belfast

The Journey

It was a frosty morning, everything was quiet.
Suddenly a pair of eyes came roaring up the road.
It came closer and closer. It stopped beside me. It
hissed at me. I was lured in. 'Return to Belfast,' I
asked the bus driver. I went and sat down.

William Frizelle (11)
Campbell College, Belfast

Murder On The Plain

The lion stalked his prey in the night, like a
possessed hypnotist.
The wildebeest was blissfully unaware of death
knocking on his door. As the lion got closer, the
winds were changing. He wasted no time. Poised,
like a spring, the lion leapt through the air, his
hunger leaving carnage.

Charlie Edgar (12)
Campbell College, Belfast

The Baby's Journey Upstairs

The baby was lurking through the mist, until he found the stairs. The tip-tap was like a drain dripping, but the baby was going upstairs. He didn't stop until he reached the top. After, he said to himself, 'I want to do this again!'

Jack Boal (12)
Campbell College, Belfast

Gangsta's Paradise

I felt top of the world! Nobody could catch me,
not even the fuzz, 'cause I'm a gangster! Running
through alleys, abandoned houses all boarded up,
with my gun held high.
'Freeze …'
My heart stopped as I heard guns being loaded. I
spat tobacco out and turned to face them …

James Boyle (11)
Campbell College, Belfast

The War

It was 1936. We were invading the Japanese Empire. Then there was a flash, *bang!* Then, *'Ambush!'* They ran out of their bunkers with bayonets. Then I was stabbed by the enemy and as my light was going out, my bedroom light was going on.
'Jack, time for school, honey!'

Jack Gault (11)
Campbell College, Belfast

The Barber's

I walked into the barber's to see red blood everywhere. The victim, still alive. I walked out slowly, but the barber said, 'Sorry about the dye, how much hair do you want off?' The sense of relief was phenomenal. That's why I hate the barbers.

Kyle Martin (11)
Campbell College, Belfast

De-Ragon

The great fire-breathing beast flew over the
town, striking fear into the people's hearts and
the warning bell was ringing.
The army was firing up hundreds of arrows at him
and hit his diamond-hard skin, but one hit a red
spot on his chest and he died!

Jack Wright (11)
Campbell College, Belfast

Ghostly Wood

I decided to go for a walk one autumn day to a new forest far away. I was walking along quite happily, when I heard the crunching of leaves behind me. I turned around suddenly, to find a horrible being following me. I screamed but my cries were not heard.

Ben Taylor (11)
Campbell College, Belfast

Haircut ...

'A little trim please,' I said as I sat down. I heard
the hum of the hairdryer and my eyes closed.
Snip, snip, zzz!
'There you are, Sir, how's that?'
My eyes sprang open, I jumped and I looked in
the mirror. Harry Hill stared back at me!

Nicholas McMinn (12)
Campbell College, Belfast

Jump

My eyes … dribbling with pain. The torrential rain
was storming. The thunder pounded like a racing
heart. I was on Forth Bridge with rusty nails and
glistening iron rods surrounding me. I'd a steel
ball at the back of my throat. I was finding it hard
to breathe. I jumped.

Joshua McNeill (11)
Campbell College, Belfast

The Alien

A crackling noise is what he heard, like fire, near
and as a hunter, that was bad. As he approached
the crackling noise, something knocked him over
and he was fired at. He quickly rolled out of the
way and shot his 32 calibre rifle and watched it
drop dead.

Henry Moore (12)
Campbell College, Belfast

World Domination

It was a peaceful day in New York, until the Mario Bros jumped out of a green pipe and started to destroy the world. Little did they know, PEACE team had a plan. As the brothers were jumping on Cape Town, they detonated a bomb, which blew them into space.

Harry Kyle (12)
Campbell College, Belfast

Slamming Desks

He sat bolt upright in his uncomfortable chair,
in the austere room. A cold sweat covered his
forehead as he clutched the decrepit desk. The
woman marched up and slammed a sheet of
paper in front of him. She beamed suddenly,
'Congratulations! Highest in the class … again.'
He sighed, heavily.

Thomas Wilson (15)
Campbell College, Belfast

Untitled

One day Josh was on the beach. He found a dead shark. He took it home and cooked it. 'Yum,' he said, as he gobbled it down. Then suddenly the cooker caught on fire. He dialled 999 and they were there very, very quickly. 'Thank you very much,' he said.

Thomas Lindsay (12)
Campbell College, Belfast

The Struggle In The Sea

It was thrashing, struggling for air. It was a matter of life and death. There were turquoise blisters on my hands, grasping the metal pole that would decide the fate of the poor mammal that was fighting for its life. I had to try, or my dad would die.

Niall Burton (13)
Campbell College, Belfast

The Cheese Monster

It was coming for me! It was twice my speed and it had cheese! I was running my bum off, jumping over everything. I was sprinting down the hall in school, jumping down the stairs and all of a sudden, I felt a crack and fell to the floor. *'Help!'*

Curtis Brady (13)
Campbell College, Belfast

The Circus

There were juggling balls flying everywhere. One
minute there was a unicycle on my toe, the next,
it was balancing on my chin. It was bonkers! From
acrobats swinging through the air from trapeze to
trapeze, to clowns dancing upside down and *bam!*
It was all over, that's a show!

Ronan Jenkinson (12)
Campbell College, Belfast

The Prey

The assassin chased his prey through the city, swerving one way and another. The assassin, a sword in one hand and death in the other, sprinted. The prey, a noble who killed peasants for fun, wasn't having fun, as he came to a dead end. The assassin finished the noble.

Chris Orr (13)
Campbell College, Belfast

Harry The Hippo

Hello, my name is Harry the Hippo. I'm going to the beach to meet my friends. Later on, we are going to play volleyball. Afterwards, we are going for a cool, relaxing swim and then later on tonight, I am going to watch some television at Chris the Crab's house.

Luke Johnston (12)
Campbell College, Belfast

The Vending Machine

Another day in the vending machine. *Ooh*, a person has come. *Noooo!* Not my best friend, Eb, the chocolate Fredo. Who will I talk to now? Here's another ugly face coming over. He has put in 50p. That's what I'm worth. Why am I moving? No, don't bite me!

Thomas Watson (13)
Campbell College, Belfast

No Time To Rest

Our two heroes do not have time to rest. The Bionic Booger Boys are back! This time they seem to have grown. The heroes run at the Booger Boys, determined to win this time. They aim for the hearts of the Boogers, killing them. Our heroes are safe for now ...

Peter Hughes (12)
Campbell College, Belfast

Playing Billiards

The black ball was surrounded by yellow and red balls. A white ball was hit at the group and scattered the balls in all directions. A red ball went in a pocket. Then another red ball was hit by this white ball. Soon there were no more black balls left.

Sebastian Haley (13)
Campbell College, Belfast

An Adventure Of Sackboy

There he was, Sackboy. The witch had spoken of treasure beyond these fire rocks. He jumped over them, but suddenly, through the ground, grew a fire flower, well known in these parts of the collector's lair. He was no match. He fell, defeated at the plant's roots.

Israel Corry (12)
Campbell College, Belfast

Untitled

The beast was running like lightning and the werewolf was chasing it in an instant. They both stopped dead on the spot and suddenly ran as fast the other way. We all knew what had happened. The end had finally come. We all knew that Supernovality was doomed again.

Ben Middlesworth (12)
Campbell College, Belfast

A Killer Encounter

I did the best I could to avoid its killer claws and teeth. I darted from hallway to hallway, hearing the thud of its heavy body. I saw it. I tried to get away, but I fell and sprained my ankle and then I saw it come closer, closer, closer ...

Daniel Kealey (12)
Campbell College, Belfast

The Anonymous Incident

Joe lived alone. His family wanted to relocate
him to a 'Fold'. Moving furniture, they found a
secret room. Suddenly Joe screamed! A shroud of
darkness appeared; there was silence …
In the darkness of the sombre night, the isolated
cottage merged with the surroundings and
disappeared into the eerie shadows.

James Lavery (13)
Campbell College, Belfast

Untitled

They ran through the forest, fishing poles slapping against their backs. They ran as fast as possible, each trying desperately to edge past the other. They looked around and seeing a suitable tree, began to climb. They sat at the very top, laughing and smiling. But the bears could climb ...

Ryan Yeates (14)
Campbell College, Belfast

A Day In The Life Of Curtis Matthew Skipp!

Hello, my name is Curtis and welcome to my
world. I wake up in the morning. I go to school.
When I come home from school, I do homework.
After homework, I have dinner with my family.
Then I get rather tired and up to my bed to sleep.
Yawn!

Curtis Skipp (14)
Campbell College, Belfast

Just The Shop

Andrew and Michael were going out of the school
ground with their fellow muckers to the shop.
On entering the shop, they came across a delight,
such as a Wispa Gold chocolate bar. It put such
delight on their faces that they screamed and
shouted with their caramel filled mouths!

Andrew Porter (14)
Campbell College, Belfast

SAS In Trouble

He joined the SAS in 1984. He was involved in numerous operations with the regiment. He was in a squad of eight. They were known as 'dangerous'. They had to blow up a fuel station, but unfortunately they were all caught in the explosion. They will always be called 'dangerous'.

Scott Irwin-Houston (14)
Campbell College, Belfast

Waiting For ...

In the middle of nowhere, Joe waited for the connecting bus to his new life and civilisation. It had been a blisteringly hot day. As dusk fell, the ground and air cooled. It brought a welcome relief. Something brushed his face. A sharp stinging pressure to his throat. Lights out.

Rhys Stewart (13)
Campbell College, Belfast

The Best Story In The World Man, Yeah!

As I walked down a very, very steep, steep, long, long and bumpy road, I saw my friend wearing a long, long blue T-shirt, which said, 'Go Bulls! Go Bulls!' When I reached him, I said, 'Why is your blue, blue top so big on you, my friend?'
'Don't know.'

Max Thallon (14)
Campbell College, Belfast

Jimmy The Whale

Jimmy the whale was swimming in the ocean. One day, he saw an odd-looking fish. It was a big, black fish, with flippers on the end of its legs. But fish don't have legs! He swam really quickly, but then he saw it was a diver studying fish!

Matt Russell (11)
Campbell College, Belfast

Jimmy The Squirrel

Once upon a time there was a boy called Jimmy. Jimmy lived with his mum and dad. On his eleventh birthday, he was abducted by aliens. This was a big shock for Jimmy's parents. The aliens tested on him for months and finally he returned, only he was a … squirrel!

Lewis Allan (11)
Campbell College, Belfast

Was It Just A Dream?

Matthew's eyes darted open. His heart was pounding. He kept saying to himself, 'It was just a dream! But those aliens had seemed so real!' He got dressed and went downstairs for breakfast. The house was eerily quiet. He stepped outside and looked up and saw the aliens departing.
'Help!'

James Kissock (12)
Campbell College, Belfast

Untitled

Our dog had eaten rat poison from the farm two fields away from us. We had to take her to the vet.
We got a call in the morning and she'd survived.
We went to pick her up and she looked very happy. We went home and wrapped her up.

Chris Megahey (11)
Campbell College, Belfast

A Dog Called Bucky

Bucky belonged to a family who were very cruel to him. He was badly beaten and neglected. One day his family threw him out into the cold. It turned out to be his lucky day. He met a boy who took pity on him and took him home.

Corey Norwood (12)
Campbell College, Belfast

Untitled

This summer I went to Majorca. It was amazing.
I'll never forget the food, the views, town and my
hotel. The sun was blazing, but we didn't give up,
we wanted to get around just about everything. If
we made it, so could you. Alcudia has everything.
Non-stop entertainment.

Cameron Brady (11)
Campbell College, Belfast

Golifer

This saga is of a devious wizard called Golifer
who liked to cast spells and evil curses, causing
catastrophes.
When his underground lair was destroyed, he lost
his magic powers and was cursed to work hard as
a farmer for his eternity, learning that true power
is not magic based.

Benjamin Tweedie (12)
Campbell College, Belfast

Assassins Creed 2

As I came out of the darkness and into the moonlight, I noticed in the corner of my eye, I knew I had found my target. I jumped over to his balcony. He turned his back and I opened the door. He was dead in a flash.

Jeffrey Taylor (11)
Campbell College, Belfast

Untitled

I saw the glistening sun on the edge of the town,
but suddenly, there was a shake. I could hear the
ocean. I said to my mother, 'Listen, Mum, can you
hear that?' Then I heard a scream. I saw a huge
wave. It wiped out the whole town.

Jack Howard (12)
Campbell College, Belfast

Untitled

Do you ever wonder if there's another universe?
Well, there is! Each time you make a decision, you
create another universe, so people find gateways
to other worlds. Someone once wanted to
destroy a universe, because he'd been mocked,
but he needed a wonderful, speed of light,
unpredictable missile … oops!

Louis Pinkerton (12)
Campbell College, Belfast

The Dinner Line

The class ends. I'm set free. I dart out. I dash down the hallway. I duck and swerve, determined to get to the front of the dinner line. I fly around the corner. Only two people there. I devour my feast. Back to class to wait for the next feast.

Keelan McCarthy (12)
Campbell College, Belfast

Noises In The Town

Her footsteps stamped off the bus loudly. As she moved through the crowd, the hustle-bustle began to hurt her ears. She covered them up to drown out the loud noise. Christmas music sounded along with her loud voice, calling me. Then I realised Mum had gone Christmas shopping.

Adam McGowan (12)
Campbell College, Belfast

The Old Sweet Shop

The old sweet shop, what wonder awaits inside. Look at all that old candy on the window sill, waiting to be eaten. Like the sour strawberry suckers or that giant gummy bear that was never bought. But why does it never open? Why is all the candy still in there?

Timothy Nelson (12)
Campbell College, Belfast

Indecision

The boy walked into the restaurant. He had a problem; he couldn't decide what to order! Then he decided to flip a coin. It landed - heads. So he ordered a cheeseburger and chips. They took a while to arrive, but tasted wonderful! He paid the waitress and left for home.

Josh Harbinson (12)

Campbell College, Belfast

The Secret Watch

Jane was in the woods. She had found a pocket watch. It said in it, 'To Mary from John'. As soon as she said, 'John,' the pocket watch sprung to life and started ticking. She opened it and a bright shining light appeared. She closed her eyes, 'I'm scared.' *Poof!*

Ethan Hunsdale (13)
Campbell College, Belfast

Goal!

There are three minutes left in the European Cup Final between Liverpool and Barcelona. It is 0-0. Rafa looks to his bench, finding Aquilani, still half-fit, Rafa brings him on. It is the last attack of the match. There's a free-kick. Aquilani steps up, he shoots … *goal!*

Cameron Mills (13)

Campbell College, Belfast

Gun Down

Three American soldiers go behind enemy lines and save hostages from Germany. They use fake IDs and uniforms to get past the Germans to kill Adolf Hitler without mercy. Unfortunately, everything does not go to plan and they face some difficult moments, but luck is on their side to victory!

Curt Douglas (13)
Campbell College, Belfast

Cultra Rules

While Bob was walking down the Cultra Road,
in the midst of the fresh, breezy air, there was a
roaring of a large bang of a K95 pistol. Everyone
was shocked at the unbelievable sight of the
incident.
Later on there was a police car that cleaned up
the problem.

Cori Lee Hamill (13)
Campbell College, Belfast

A Stab In The Dark

He crept through the door, as silent as the deep black of the night. His blade glinted in the silver moonlight. He slashed out, the blood splattering against the wall. He clamped his hand over the victim's mouth before lowering the body to the ground and melting into the shadows.

Alistair Bissett (12)
Campbell College, Belfast

Intergalactic Bunny And Hamster Wars

Long ago, in a galaxy far, far away, a new era began. Luke Carrotcruncher battled the Dark Lord, Obi-Ham(ster) Kenobi. Obi-Ham attacked Luke, slicing his carrot in half. Then tables turned as Luke landed a powerful punch and defeated Obi-Ham by making him eat the carrot.

Andrew Rankin (13)
Campbell College, Belfast

Untitled

The lion had escaped from its cage. The guards hadn't noticed this. The cat crept towards the guards. The guards still not knowing it had escaped. The vicious lion bit the first guard. The other guard noticed this, tried to escape, but the lion chased him and killed everyone else.

Michael Simpson (13)
Campbell College, Belfast

Over The Top

I was frightened, with bullets flying over my head,
with the sound of a rifle's rapid rattle. When
we got the order from our General, we hastily
maneuvered over the top, keeping close to the
ground, shielding our bodies with men being
taken out one by one. *'Argh!* I'm next!'

Matthew Rodgers (12)
Campbell College, Belfast

The Eagle's Nest

Tahir galloped through the valley as swift as an eagle, his eyes locked onto his prey. He charged, swinging his saber all around him, heading for the flag. His prey fell, Tahir jumped like an eagle on its prey and secured the flag and then returned to his nest, Alamut.

Joshua Catherall (12)
Campbell College, Belfast

The Trolls

The girl walked down a long, dark road. She felt scared. She heard a noise. Then something black jumped out of the bushes. She tried to run away, but the trolls caught her and put her on the ground. It felt like a nightmare. She was left screaming, 'Help!'

Amy Tweedie (11)
Downshire Secondary School, Carrickfergus

The Day I Met An Alien

One day I was walking down the street, when I saw something black and blue, with big eyes. It started to move. I started to feel worried, scared, nervous. I saw more. It was orange as well. I wanted to go over, so I went over. It was an alien!

Chloe Smyth (12)
Downshire Secondary School, Carrickfergus

The Biscuit And The Teacup

I was waiting in silence, shaking with fear. The cup was sitting there, the kettle was boiling and all of a sudden the button went *ping!* A giant person came in and lifted the kettle with scalding water coming out. Suddenly I rose into the air and dunked into tea.

Lauren Patterson (11)
Downshire Secondary School, Carrickfergus

The Try Line

The floodlights hitting my face, my heart pounding faster than ever, my teammates were puffed out. I began to run. My team behind me, I felt the hot breath on my neck. I was sliding - then ... *score!* The fans at Ravenhill roared. First victory of the season! *Yes!*

Scott Molloy (12)
Downshire Secondary School, Carrickfergus

Waiting For The Gunfire

On the blocks, shaking with excitement, waiting
for the gun. So nervous. *Bang!* I catapulted out
of my blocks, the crowd roaring, other racers
breathing behind me. I saw the finish line in front
of me. Legs pumping, arms moving, heart rising -
first place! I felt so proud of myself.

Hollie McArthur (12)
Downshire Secondary School, Carrickfergus

The Land Of The Dragons

Late one night I was playing games and got sucked
inside to a land of dragons. I fell on my face and
a light blue dragon was staring at me. It froze my
crew. Then a big green dragon appeared in front
of me.
To be continued ...

Jonathan Reid (12)
Downshire Secondary School, Carrickfergus

The Day I Won The Race

My heart started to pump as the man started to talk. I got my feet in place. The gun fired. I heard the sound of the gun in my head and I bolted. The crowd started to cheer and I accelerated. Yes! I won and the crowd cheered much louder!

Sarah McNickle (11)
Downshire Secondary School, Carrickfergus

Bang!

It was Halloween and it was a cold night, when Jack was on his way home from his friend's. He started to make his way through the forest and then he heard a snap. Suddenly a dark figure started running towards him. Jack ran! *Bang!* There was silence …

Ross Nelson (13)
Downshire Secondary School, Carrickfergus

The Small, Short Figure

It was a cold, windy night. The boy stared at it!
It was a small, short figure. The figure whispered
something. The boy sprinted to his bedroom in
terror, shaken by this strange figure he had seen.
He heard strange noises!
He was suddenly woken by his alarm clock!

Megan Elliott (12)
Downshire Secondary School, Carrickfergus

The Loch Ness Monster

We were in a small rowing boat in the middle of
the loch, when my father shouted, 'You caught
something!' and grabbed the rod. When he did
so, the whole boat tipped, *splash!* And the water
calmed.
What happened in Loch Ness that day changed
our lives forever.

Tony Clark (13)
Downshire Secondary School, Carrickfergus

The Haunted House

It was Halloween night and Ashley was out with her friends. They went to an abandoned house. They decided to go up the stairs because they heard something and wanted to see what it was. It was getting louder. They ran! But when they came out, Ashley wasn't there!

Danielle Aicken (12)
Downshire Secondary School, Carrickfergus

The Cave!

Jack was being followed so he ran into a cave. Jack went deeper into the cave. He could hear screaming, so he kept going. The voices were getting closer. Jack ran, but he tripped. The croaking voice came closer and said … 'My throat's sore, can I have a Strepsil?'

Stuart Andrews (12)
Downshire Secondary School, Carrickfergus

Horror Holiday

'I'm going exploring!' shouted Joe. Joe and his family were at the beach on their holidays. Joe pulled back the reeds and there was a sandy path. Joe walked along it for miles. He found nothing, until … something caught his eyes. *'Argh!'* he screamed. It was a dead body.

Philip Buchanan (13)
Downshire Secondary School, Carrickfergus

The Boy And His Rich Grandmother's Haunted Mansion

There once was a boy called Ronald, he was visiting his rich grandmother for the first time. When he saw her house it was a scary mansion. He went through the gates to the door. The door was open and he went in. Then he felt something at his legs ...

Matthew Brown (13)
Downshire Secondary School, Carrickfergus

World War II

I turned round and my best friend fell to the ground - his eyes wide open. People were screaming so loud it was unbearable. I ran through all the blood to help other people. Before I got there, I heard a loud noise. All of a sudden it went completely silent.

Rebecca Crossett (13)
Downshire Secondary School, Carrickfergus

The Haunted School

Everyone knew about Monty Reynolds. A pupil called John always knew about the ghost Monty and never believed it. He decided to go into school at night with his friend, Monty. Monty disappeared and John started to get scared. He walked into a maths room and never came back out.

Jamie Brennan (13)
Downshire Secondary School, Carrickfergus

The Execution

And so the day has come, the day of the execution. The man walks up to the stand. He kneels down and so the axe is lifted and brought down on his neck. Then after the crowd walk away, he stands up and walks around, looking for his head.

Daniel Colligan (13)
Downshire Secondary School, Carrickfergus

Graves

I'm Susan. I'm dead. Well, not really ... I'll start from the beginning. I never really respected the dead and one day I accidentally kicked a football at a grave. The person in the grave killed me ... What is that annoying noise up there? Better put him in his grave.

Serin Campbell (12)
Downshire Secondary School, Carrickfergus

Tick-Tock

Tom was watching Scooby-Doo. He switched it off and realised none of the clocks worked.
'Mum, none of the clocks work.'
'I know, darling, they've been like that for ages. Let's just go to church,' replied Mum.
Tom came home and all he could hear … *tick-tock, tick-tock!*

Karris Giani (13)
Downshire Secondary School, Carrickfergus

Magic Pants

I got new pants today, but I bought them from a gypsy camp for £5. The woman who sold me them said they were magic pants. I got home and tried them on and I flew! I hit my head on the roof, so I'm not wearing those again!

Jake Gardner (13)
Downshire Secondary School, Carrickfergus

The Last Chance

One night, me, Kennedy and Paddy all went into the forest for a sleepover. We all walked down to the haunted cabin and this guy walked out and tried to kill us. So we ran and Paddy fell, so she was killed. Me and Kennedy ran back home.

Zoey Hanley (13)
Downshire Secondary School, Carrickfergus

Future Dream

A boy called Paul came home from school, very tired. So he lay down and fell asleep. He appeared in the street. It looked the same, but he soon figured out that the people were robots. They started trying to kill him, but he killed them first with a gun.

Amy Craig (13)
Downshire Secondary School, Carrickfergus

The Five Crazy Bulls

Me and my friends go to see a rodeo, bull riding and bucking broncos. There's a guy called Bolton. He asks me and my friends if we would like a go at riding the bulls. We will never forget the thrill of riding the bulls. Our bodies still hurt.

Philip Magill (12)
Downshire Secondary School, Carrickfergus

My Magical Holiday

I was at a caravan site with my mum and dad.
'It's nearly 10pm. Are you going to bed yet?'
I said, 'Yes.' I got into bed and went to sleep. I got
up again and everything was different. Suddenly I
was in everyone's dreams.
I wonder what happens next?

Courtney-Leigh Owens (12)
Downshire Secondary School, Carrickfergus

Two In Love

One day Katy was walking along the beach, when
she saw this hunk walking her way. He came to
ask her something.
'Hi, I'm Eddy, will you go out with me?'
'Oh, yes!' said Katy.
So they walked along the beach and lived happily
ever after together.

Katy Baird (12)
Downshire Secondary School, Carrickfergus

Nightmare

Adam stayed up too long, so he went to bed. He looked round and saw a ghost standing there. It had a hatchet. It took a swing at Adam, nearly hit him, but it missed. It tried again and missed again. Adam woke up, shouting loudly and crying, very scared.

Jordan Hunter (13)
Downshire Secondary School, Carrickfergus

The Day I Got A New Car

One day I'd just bought my new flying car and it was good. Then I was flying along. *Crash!* I had crashed into a flying bike and it was a wee boy driving it, he was about eight years old and he said, 'Sorry, man!'

Joshua Reynolds (12)
Downshire Secondary School, Carrickfergus

The Day Aliens Came To School

I was sitting in English. There was a knock at the door. Miss said, 'Come in!' We heard footsteps, but couldn't see anyone. Miss screamed and ran away, after green aliens appeared. They said that they were going to take over the world. With a lot of trouble, they did.

Katrina Dillon (13)
Downshire Secondary School, Carrickfergus

My Dream

My dream was about me. I was on my horse and I got lost. I was scared. I was all alone. Then I was walking and found a castle. I went inside. I saw a dragon, wizards, ghosts and princesses. I thought, *where am I?* I kept walking. My dream finished.

Erin Hamilton (12)
Downshire Secondary School, Carrickfergus

Horror At Midnight

Going on holiday to a haunted house. when they got there, they went straight to bed and the two children heard a bang downstairs and they went to investigate and in the kitchen, there was a man with a chainsaw and he cut the heads off and they died.

Isaac Kirker (13)
Downshire Secondary School, Carrickfergus

Pixie Path

There was a long, dark and bendy path through the forest. Samantha and I walked slowly down the path. Suddenly, we saw little people running into the bushes. We ran over behind them and peeked our small heads through the thick bushes. In front of our eyes were pixies, dancing.

Gemma McArthur (12)
Downshire Secondary School, Carrickfergus

The Land Of Nightmare

Jim was coming home from Bradd's house. Gareth and a clown were beating up a brick house with a melted wooden sphere. Jim threw a block of pasta at them and a luminous blob attacked Jim with a glow stick. He ran away and died, because of custard brain poisoning.

Bradd Johnston (13)
Downshire Secondary School, Carrickfergus

Crazy Times

A giant ice cream flew into a tree and hit a cat.
Then it turned into a pear slice and a clown
popped out of a bush and flew on a kangaroo to
the moon. Crazy times.

Rory Magill (13)
Downshire Secondary School, Carrickfergus

Monster Man

I am walking down the street and I take a short cut. It is a dark alley and suddenly a monster comes out of a hedge and he takes off his mask ... and then my alarm goes. I am awake, but I have no legs!

John Lavery (12)
Downshire Secondary School, Carrickfergus

The Day In The Life Of A Horse

Today is my day, my time to shine. My owner
Lucy is show jumping at the UK Under 15
Championships. We are heading to the jumping
ground. I hope we will win, Lucy is the best rider
in Northern Ireland and I am the best horse.

Ellie McConnell (12)
Downshire Secondary School, Carrickfergus

Random

A giant watermelon-flavoured, coconut-shaped cucumber fell from space. It landed right on top of Steven Jello's new house. Thankfully, Steve was out. Out of the cucumber came a giant jelly-flavoured anaconda called Jermaine. He ate Cardboard City and exploded into a cola cube!

Jamie McCracken (13)

Downshire Secondary School, Carrickfergus

Splash!

I was on a plane. I was just about to jump on the count of three. One, two, three, jump! *'Argh!'* I had no parachute. I landed in the sea. *Splash!* I woke up and found myself in the bath. It must have all been a dream.

Emily Brownlee (12)

Downshire Secondary School, Carrickfergus

Bang!

Slowly, the bully walked up to me. *Thump, thump, thump!* He hit me and I was just standing there, bloody and sore. I walked over to a teacher and reported the boy for assaulting me. The teacher yelled at him and he never did hassle me again. Never ever again!

Gemma Sparkes (13)
Downshire Secondary School, Carrickfergus

The Hockey Final

There I was, running down the wing, as fast as I could go. It was the final of the high schools' cup. The score was 0-0. If we did not score, we would have to share the cup. I hit the ball into the centre-mid. She scored!

Gabrielle Thompson (13)
Downshire Secondary School, Carrickfergus

Hero Or Villain?

This was it. All that stood between me and victory, was a goalkeeper and two posts. If I hit this right, I'd be a hero. Hit it wrong, then I'd be remembered as a villain. I hit the ball with all my strength and watched it fly into the corner.

Roger Wilson (13)
Downshire Secondary School, Carrickfergus

It

Thud, thud! went the pulse in her ears. Eyes on
it. Its eyes flaming. Stumbling, she jumped up.
Tripping, falling, trembling with fear, it pounced.
She crawled, scrambled, unable to feel her body.
Looking up, its teeth gleaming closer, closer.
Mouth wide. *Thud, thud!* went the pulse in her
ears.

Chloe Thompson (13)
Downshire Secondary School, Carrickfergus

Santa Is True

Thump! I woke up. *Thump!* I clambered out of
bed. *Thump!*
Santa? I wondered. I rushed downstairs.
'No, no, no!' sighed Santa. He clicked his fingers.
He disappeared. I watched out the window. I
searched for a clue, but I can tell you now, Santa
is true. His reindeer too.

Rebecca Stronge (13)
Downshire Secondary School, Carrickfergus

Losing Teeth With Clumsy Bella

Flutter! Flutter! Bella was on her way, with a coin for little Emily who lost her first tooth. While she was putting the money under her pillow, she woke. 'Shh! little girl and go back to sleep.' Bella was only here exchanging her teeth for money to save for sweets.

Wendy Ritchie (13)
Downshire Secondary School, Carrickfergus

The Schoolchild

Out of breath, panting while struggling to catch his breath, it was the lonely child late for school again. The only sound he could hear, was the smacking of his shoes hitting the ground and the school bell signaling the start of classes. *'Nooo!* I'm late again! I'm so grounded!'

William Surgeoner (13)
Downshire Secondary School, Carrickfergus

Scary Noises

I was walking down the road when it happened. I heard something calling my name. It sounded like the wind. I started to run. It sounded as it followed me. My heart was thumping. I was really scared now. Suddenly I was tackled to the ground by my friend.

Bradley Young (14)
Downshire Secondary School, Carrickfergus

Do Not Speed On A Road Or This May Happen To You

He is driving down the road at 120mph. Suddenly,
a dog runs onto the road. He swerves, skids,
slides. The car rolls down the road and crashes
straight into a lamp post.
He wakes up in hospital with a broken body and a
speeding ticket.

Andrew Rodgers (14)
Downshire Secondary School, Carrickfergus

The Derby Stallion

It was the great Derby race. All the horses lined up in the starting box. *Bang!* The gun was fired. The horses galloped, running with all their power. In seconds they were all out running for first place. You could hear the crowd go wild as each horse jumped.

Clare Magowan (14)
Downshire Secondary School, Carrickfergus

The Butcher

I walked into my local butcher's, where the meat
was on sale. 'These disappearances are terrible!'
he said.
It was the third this week. I ate my dinner. It
tasted weird. I walked to my friend's. I was
grabbed from behind. Oh no! It was the butcher!

Steven Kissick (14)
Magherafelt High School, Magherafelt

Ghostly Goings-On

Wsshe! Woo! This house must be haunted. The doors creak, the windows crash together making a horrific sound. Windows are broken, making curtains blow. I hear a tapping noise upstairs, like someone is there, but I won't go up! I can't go up! It might be a ghost!

Matthew Nesbitt (13)
Magherafelt High School, Magherafelt

Holiday Adventures

I'm on a beach in Spain. It's so warm. There are
few or no clouds. The sand is extra warm. The
noise of the sea would make you sleep. The
water is warmer than the sand. I haven't been
here before. I would come again. This is a holiday
adventure.

Reuben Caskey (13)
Magherafelt High School, Magherafelt

The Ghost Of Loughrey Lane

Walking down the lane, past the haunted house. Hearing a very loud and terrifying noise coming from the top right window. Looking up, seeing a white figure gliding past the window. Suddenly everything went quiet. Black out. Standing beside us was the ghost of Loughrey Lane. Petrified, we scurried home!

Dean Martin (13)
Magherafelt High School, Magherafelt

Untitled

Night before Halloween. Children excited at dressing up. Timothy was a very lonely boy. Everyone called him Lonely Timmy. Timmy was alone in his house. Kids were ringing on his doorbell, playing tricks, but Timmy was clever. Door creaked open and out came Timmy, eyes wide, holding a knife!

Zuzana Sarkoziova (14)
Magherafelt High School, Magherafelt

The Dolphins And The Shark

I am in the water, learning to be a lifeguard, when suddenly a shark starts to swim around me. I start screaming, 'Help! Help!' but nobody hears. Then suddenly four dolphins start swimming round me in circles and the shark disappears. Then the dolphins disappear and I swim back.

Victoria Moore (15)

Magherafelt High School, Magherafelt

What Was That?

It was coming! Its great height was terrifying! Its long hair as slimy as slug trails and a face as round as a cake. It wore big pink dungarees. It roared in pain as it crashed to the ground. It was like an earthquake.
'I want my tricycle!' she screamed.

Kelly Ewing (13)
Magherafelt High School, Magherafelt

Angel!

I see him clearly. He is so cool. He sings like an angel and looks like an angel, with beautiful hair and dance moves. I feel all tense, as I look at him. He looks back at me and smiles. He is Aston from JLS and he's the best dressed!

Charlene Burnett (13)
Magherafelt High School, Magherafelt

A Historical Event

I was so tired my eyes hurt! It was the same
thing every morning, as I got to work. My eyelids
were so heavy. I fell asleep. I got roped in. I got
wrapped around the driving staff, swung around,
thrown into the bottles. There was a bang.
I'm dead.

William McMaster (13)
Magherafelt High School, Magherafelt

The Deadly Snake

We had been lost for endless days in the deep, green undergrowth of the deadly Amazon forest. Suddenly, a brightly coloured snake stopped us in our tracks. This guy was looking me dead in the eye. I was suddenly relieved when he slithered away slowly, towards the tall tree.

Jonathan Nesbitt (14)
Magherafelt High School, Magherafelt

Fish Tales

I was swimming around my little fish tank like any other day. My owners were away and I had got bored because no other fish were here, because the last one had died and had been flushed down the toilet! Suddenly, I got sucked into the machine that blew bubbles!

Alex Hutchinson (13)
Magherafelt High School, Magherafelt

Hyper Hippos

We went to the zoo and I wanted to see the hippos. The time I was there, the hippos were so shy, but today they were going mad. You were able to go out on a boat to see them, but they were so hyper, they capsized the boat!

Mark Miller (13)
Magherafelt High School, Magherafelt

Ghostly Goings-On

It was a dark, long day, when I heard a strange noise coming from the living room. My great granny had died just a few weeks before. My sisters came and listened to the strange noise. We walked in and to our surprise, there was the ghost of our granny!

Shannon Hutchinson (14)
Magherafelt High School, Magherafelt

It All Started With An Injury

The alarm had sounded. I had to get on duty.
There was someone injured on the motorway.
We paramedics had to help. We were flying down
the motorway, when a car flew in front of us!
Crash! We were overturned!
Next thing I knew, they were treating me in
hospital!

Grace Nesbitt (13)
Magherafelt High School, Magherafelt

The Gamer

It was the middle of the night. I woke up to strange noises. I climbed out of bed and crept out to the landing. As I slowly walked to the top of the stairs, I heard my brother shouting, 'No!' I ran downstairs. My brother was playing Xbox games - again!

Terri Holgate (14)
Magherafelt High School, Magherafelt

Vampire Death

They say, back in the day, that the only way to get rid of a vampire, was to stake it through the heart, stuff the body with garlic, burn them to ashes and scatter them in a river, so that they wouldn't come back to get you.

Morery Stewart (13)
Magherafelt High School, Magherafelt

The Birthday Outfit

It was my 13th birthday. My family and friends were coming, so it was going to be brilliant. I was talking to my friends, when I noticed someone was wearing the same dress as me. I was ready to start a fight, when I realised it was my gran. Embarrassing!

Jodie Evans (13)
Magherafelt High School, Magherafelt

Scary Halloween!

It was Halloween night. I was at home when all of a sudden, the power went off. I was alone and I smelt smoke. There was a bang in the house. There was a fire and the smoke was terrible. What was I going to do? Remember, I was alone.

Joanne Brown (13)
Magherafelt High School, Magherafelt

Midnight Walk

Walking along the narrow road, feeling cold in the midnight wind, sprinkling down my spine, leaves missing off trees, dancing upon my feet, keeping my hand clutched inside my pockets, scared of Jack Frost stealing my warmth. Birds laughing, chattering, making me feel I'm being watched by shadows behind me.

Laura Patton (13)
Magherafelt High School, Magherafelt

In The Vet's

How much longer was I going to wait? The sweat was pouring from my brow. My heart was pounding. Dogs were barking. Cats were miaowing. The clock was ticking. I was pacing up and down. Then suddenly … Bailey came out from the vet's, happy and healthy.

Alix Szeremeta (14)
Magherafelt High School, Magherafelt

The Big Game

His teammate passed him the ball and then he sprinted towards the opponent's goal, dribbling past every oncoming defender. He then kicked the ball with all his strength and it went over the goalkeeper's head and into the back of the net. The crowd were ecstatic with joy. *Goal!*

Kyle Moore (13)
Magherafelt High School, Magherafelt

Yes Or No!

Singing, dancing, performing, that's what they always do. Trying to win the hearts of almost everyone to get through, week by week. Yes, no, they wouldn't know.
Until one night, they would find out it wasn't to be. Runner-up would have to do, but what could they do?

Jessica Wilson (14)
Magherafelt High School, Magherafelt

The Strange Noise!

When I opened the door and went in, I could tell
that something was wrong. There were no lights
on and I heard a scraping noise to my left, as if
someone was moving furniture. I started to get
scared. Then someone came up behind me and
shouted, 'Happy birthday!'

Bethany Henry (13)
Magherafelt High School, Magherafelt

A New Friend

Today I made a new friend, but this one was the ultimate friend. He listened to all my problems, never interrupted me once. He didn't argue with me and I didn't feel judged, but when I tried to shake hands, it was nothing but my own reflection in a mirror.

Thomas Abraham (12)
Methodist College, Belfast

Graveyard

Walking through the graveyard at the dead of
night, the leaves crunch beneath his feet, he hears
a howl, jerks round fearfully. He stops … looks
around, starts to panic, palms become sweaty. His
breathing increases rapidly, as he realises that the
friend he's supposed to meet, is hanging above
him.

Zach Jordan (12)
Methodist College, Belfast

Police In The House

He was watching TV. It was 11pm. He heard something screeching. *It's only the wind,* he thought. The fire was lit and smoke billowed out of it. He was deeply asleep. When he woke up, the police were in front of him. The alarm was because of the fire!

Jakub Salkiewicz (11)
Methodist College, Belfast

Only A Joke ...

We're walking. It's a freezing day to be walking out in the snow, I'm loving it anyway. Suddenly, he stops. His face goes white. I think I see something over the hill. It disappears and I feel something touch me from behind ... it's my boyfriend *trying* to scare me!

Georgia Gilbert (12)
Methodist College, Belfast

The Real Story Of Humpty Dumpty

Yes, it starts the same. He was sitting on a brick wall. But the truth was, he didn't fall, he was shot. Who by? I hear you ask. Well, it was the star from Twinkle, Twinkle, Little Star. He was afraid of the nursery rhyme competition. I was shocked too!

Rachel Lynn (12)
Methodist College, Belfast

My Experiences As A Sailor

Water rushing through my hair. Wind blowing in my face. The captain screaming, 'Mayday! Hole in ship! Fire back crew!' *Bang!* we fired back ... we hit them in the side! We cheered loudly! We won the battle! We actually won!
'Sarah! Hurry up! We need a bath too!' Mum shouts.

Sarojani Wilson (11)
Methodist College, Belfast

Creation Of Society

Voices roaring in the dark of night. The satisfying
sound of revolution filled the air. Crushing the
bones of the oppressors. Chaos in the name
of order, destruction in the name of justice.
Promises of humanity, equality and economic
success. A new regime is born.

Mark Ormerod (16)
Rathmore Grammar School, Belfast

A Choice

Her fearful eyes widened in her pale face. Time slowed down as she waded through the air, blood pulsing slowly and thickly through her temples. Her violently shaking hands took the gun. An icy trickle of sweat slid down her back, as she laid a trembling finger on the trigger.

Claire Varini (15)

Rathmore Grammar School, Belfast

It

'It' made its way back to the place that was supposed to be home. Today had been an improvement on the horrifying previous day. The pain worsened as 'it' neared its tormentor. Would Lauren's father attack again? She felt her heart pounding in her chest. Why her? Why her?

Emma-Louise Rea (15)
Rathmore Grammar School, Belfast

World War III

It was quiet. The screaming, crying and explosions
had stopped and this was a sign, after many hours
of struggle, of their victory. They sank, exhausted
into their chairs. There was no doubt that
tomorrow it would begin again, but for now they
could relax.
Finally, the children were asleep.

Kerri Stuart (15)
Rathmore Grammar School, Belfast

Almost Near Miss

He jumped and rolled behind the wall, bullets whistled past his ears. He heard the metallic clink of a grenade nearby. He searched with his eyes for it. Everything went black. He was in hospital. He looked down and saw no bulge for toes and knees in the sheets.

Conor Totten (15)

Rathmore Grammar School, Belfast

Slow And Shotguns Win The Race

That blasted hare had dodged Joe the tortoise too many times now. Joe was fed up. Blurs of fur boomed down the track, mocking Joe's inability. *Bang!* Its ears sagged; dashes of brain disappeared. Five hours, Joe was at the finishing line, first place - guilt free.

Hannah Tracey (16)
Rathmore Grammar School, Belfast

The Mysterious Figure

The mysterious figure raised the knife high. It glistened in the dimming light. His eyes squinted and a darkening tone came over his face, as he pounced with the knife quickly upon the carrot, slicing it delicately.

John O'Neill (16)
Rathmore Grammar School, Belfast

Death On The Battlefield

The golden bullet reflected the sun, as it crossed the gloomy battlefield. Soldiers collapsed everywhere. This bullet had one destination. Young James turned around. Time slowed. He could see each revolution the bullet made. His life flashed before his eyes, the words, 'This is it!' in his head.

Connor O'Neill (16)
Rathmore Grammar School, Belfast

Inferno

The molten fire burned brightly, the flames tickled
at our sides. I knew that we were trapped. No
escape, no chance and no hope. I entered into
a quiet place in my mind. I could feel my body
relaxing. The heat started to build and finally ...
inferno, the fire engulfed ...

Christopher Morrison (16)
Rathmore Grammar School, Belfast

The Master

Plop! The thick, fresh mass of red hits the surface
and it awaits with eager impatience. Mixed with
imagination and presented on a blank, thoughtless
canvas like a delicate flower. The master checks
the water and light. Passion is something of
beauty, it's an art.

Nicole McFall (15)
Rathmore Grammar School, Belfast

Justice

I glanced at my watch, three o'clock, it was time. I took a deep breath and attempted to stop myself from shaking. I stepped out of the car, the frosty air stung my face as I walked towards the courthouse. The man who destroyed me was lead past - my husband.

Amy Tennyson (16)
Rathmore Grammar School, Belfast

The Mystery Of Cooking

The warm sticky substance bubbled and roasted
as the clan observed in fascination and complete
awe. They could not wait to see the final result.
It crackled and bubbled and began to take shape
and colour. Its aroma filled every part of the
room. Finally, the ticker rang.
'Cake's ready!'

Rachel Rogan (16)
Rathmore Grammar School, Belfast

The Chase

The roaring monster crawled after me. So I ran.
He screamed viciously, 'I will catch you!'
I tried to hide on high surfaces. He was still
present. I threw everything at him. He didn't give
up! Suddenly the monster stopped. Lying on the
floor, asleep, my little brother was defeated.

Christopher Fagan (12)
St Columb's College, Derry

Flag Farce!

The scores are level, the crowd on the edge of their seats. Our forward expertly pierces the ball through their watertight defence, keeper to beat … *goal!* We celebrate a true hero … one glance across, the linesman's flag is up - a nation's dreams destroyed!

Jack Higgins (13)
St Columb's College, Derry

Violent Night!

The surface is flat. The current slow. Together people and fish swim leisurely through the crystal clear water. Night comes quick! A storm begins. The current erupts. The sea becomes barren of life. Lightning flashes! Thunder cracks! The sea rages! Morning arrives, vanquishing the storm. All is calm … until tonight!

Garry Mallett (12)
St Columb's College, Derry

Ghostly

At the gripping speed of a Formula 1 car, it sneezed again. It was as pale as a ghost, yet greatly covered up by layers upon layers of fur and heavy cloth. Suddenly the door opened, a shiver crept down its spine. The doctor concluded, 'Only the flu.'

Thomas Chambers (12)
St Columb's College, Derry

Tick-Tock ...

Noting answers in my book, gazing at my watch,
five minutes remained. 'Hopefully we won't get
homework,' I whispered to Charlie, who was
sitting next to me.
Five more minutes elapsed. The bell rang. The
teacher - 'Homework diaries out.'
'Oh no! Homework,' I muttered, 'not again.'

Ryan Gillespie (13)
St Columb's College, Derry

Pool

He was standing on the edge, trying to get the confidence to get in the blue sea. His enemy looking round, determined to push him in. His enemy was coming round the corner! When he was almost at him, *splash!* He woke up and said, 'I'm never going swimming again.'

Ben McLaughlin (11)
St Columb's College, Derry

The Rest Was A Blank

Jimmy was alone, isolated, scared. Jimmy was running for his life, alone in the wild, he couldn't find the rest of the campers. The last thing he could remember was going out to get firewood for the camp, with his friend Mark, but the rest was a blank!

Aaron Sheerin (13)
St Columb's College, Derry

My Deathbed

I was cold, as I lay barely conscious on the floor. A man was walking towards me with a gun. He stopped in front of me. He aimed his gun at my head. My heart was racing. I held my breath. Suddenly I heard a bang and everything went black ...

Dean Moore (12)
St Columb's College, Derry

Lightning Strikes

There it stood. Perched on a rock, high up in the mountains, the lion looked around frantically for where it came from. Suddenly a bright yellow fork of lightning struck a tree in the distance, as it fell with force, smashing through a nearby house. The lion quickly scrambled off.

James McNamee (12)
St Columb's College, Derry

Area 51

Hello! One day I was a normal kid, like you. Now I'm in charge of Area 51. I was behind Roswell, JFK and the moon landing. Now as I climb Everest to get to the deactivator of the nuclear missiles, I'm the last thing that stands between good and evil!

Aodhan McCay (13)
St Columb's College, Derry

Alone

Walking along a quiet, dark road, despite the company of a full moon, I felt all alone. Suddenly, a thunderous noise shattered the quiet. I jumped ten feet into the air. Only the postman! I don't believe in ghosts or spirits! Unaware of the fading moon.

Aodhán Bradley (12)
St Columb's College, Derry

Arachnophobia

It chased me. Then it leapt onto my leg. I
screamed as loudly as I could, thinking it would
rip open my baby-tender skin. Before long, my leg
would be drenched with deep, red gashes.
My mum wildly shrieked, 'Calm down!' as she
brushed the spider from my leg.

Patrick Slevin (13)
St Columb's College, Derry

Short-Lived Glory

He emerged from his corner, bouncing
confidently, aware one punch could do it!
He clenched his fist and swung. His knuckles
pounded against his opponent's face. Everything
went still … the bell rang. He danced in glory.
The sound of his mum, 'Time for school!'
His celebrations ruined.

Paul Ferris (13)
St Columb's College, Derry

Dream On ...

It was all down to me. I simply had to score! The
pressure was on, as Kaka had scored. It was my
responsibility to put the ball in the net! I struck
the ball. It flew in. We'd won! Fantastic!
'Conor, get up now or you'll be late for school ...'

Conor Dunleavy (12)
St Columb's College, Derry

Imagination

Sean gazed at the huge shapes above. He saw a human head. A dragon and now a rhino. The fascinating sights kept his eyes fixed. 'What's this - a dog?' Sean giggled to himself, as the shapes grew more bizarre. Soon they turned back into shapeless clouds; dull and lifeless …

Rory Mullan (13)
St Columb's College, Derry

Forest Adventure

There we were. In a deep, dark, dreary forest.
Suddenly we saw a fierce flash. Terrified, we ran
off in separate directions.
Several hours later, whilst in our houses, we
received a phone call. Our friend was in hospital,
fighting for his life ...

Kieran Duffy (13)
St Columb's College, Derry

Dark Figure

I grew increasingly petrified and tearful as it drew
closer. The imposing dark figure making me jump
as it loaded up.
'This will hurt me more than it will hurt you!'
The pain was instant! Stinging and burning, the
sensation tingling.
'That's your flu jab for the year!' he remarked.

Martin Foy (12)
St Columb's College, Derry

Swift Dreams

'Get set … go!' Swift set off with the other competitors closely by his side. Ten, twenty, fifty metres, one hundred metres, he was in first place! 'Swift! Swift!' chanted the crowd. Someone tapped him on the shoulder. He turned around. Opening his eyes, his mother was waking him for school.

Rory Maguire (12)
St Columb's College, Derry

War Trauma

I was in Rio, ducking and dodging the gunfire,
looking out for the snipers shooting at me, when I
heard the loud rattle of a bomb. *Boom!*
I heard a voice call, 'Turn that game off now! Your
dinner is ready.'

Daniel Ramsay (12)
St Columb's College, Derry

Food To Die For

'I'm starving!' Ronny whimpered. Ronny gasped at the counter. There was a can. His tail waggled as he jumped up and hit the can. The can landed on Ronny. The can burst and food poured out. Ronny stared at the label, but couldn't read it. Ronny then ate the *cyanide!*

Gearoid Brady (13)
St Columb's College, Derry

The Getaway

Matthew was beginning to panic. His hands sweating, the open road loomed in front of him. He had to get away. He floored the accelerator and, wheels spinning, took off. He got less than five metres, before the engine stalled.
'Not bad for your first attempt,' said the driving instructor.

Ruaidhri O'Neill (13)
St Columb's College, Derry

The Creature

Sneaky is this creature, always sticking to the shadows. Black are his eyes, black as night, living in the sewers, hiding from us. Sharp claws, which are flexible as rubber, being caught or squashed in traps that we set. This creature that many people fear, is the rat.

Jack Gallagher (13)
St Columb's College, Derry

Ambushed!

Going through the forest, we began to hear gunshots and lots of people shouting. I thought we were in trouble. Then finally, we reached our base and had a rest. Suddenly I felt a big force. I woke up and found out a tree had fallen and knocked me out.

Riain Garcia-White (13)
St Columb's College, Derry

Bored

We were extremely bored. It started raining,
so we went to this old house. Nobody lived in
this house. We were all talking, when we heard
footsteps. At first we thought it was just next
door, but then they got louder! We left, to find
cats at the window.

Jack McKinney (13)
St Columb's College, Derry

The Chase

The policeman sprinted after the running man, who was heading towards the bus. The policeman dodged through the pedestrians and just caught the man, as he jumped on the departing bus. He grabbed the man by the shoulder and spun him around and said, 'Here Sir, you dropped your wallet.'

Tom Hickey (13)
St Columb's College, Derry

The Zombie Dance

I saw zombies everywhere. There were two
people scared out of their wits. Then one of them
turned zombie and all the zombies danced around
to a haunting song. I got scared. Then it was over.
I turned off the TV. That Michael Jackson is a
really scary guy.

Ryan Dineen (12)
St Columb's College, Derry

The Runaway Food

I was out finding food. I smelt something far away. *What's that?* I thought. Then I knew. I thought, *yum!* I got my plate and knife out of my bag. I went to get it, but he was at the bottom of the beanstalk by the time I got there.

Conor MacBride (12)
St Columb's College, Derry

The Adventures Of Madman And Stupidman

Stupidman was chasing an old woman when he was speared through bins by Madman. Stupidman fought back, he threw his blades which were dodged by Madman. Madman then went over and ate Stupidman. Madman then went over to see if the old woman was alright, and then she ate him.

Tony Cregan (12)
St Columb's College, Derry

The Murky Waters

I was in the water. We were spear fishing. The smell of blood spread in the sea. Then suddenly a dark shape appeared out of the murky darkness. It was a twenty foot long, great white shark. It charged at me.
Then I woke up.

Jason McCauley (11)
St Columb's College, Derry

The Pictures

The monster roared. I was very scared. He ripped the man's head off. 'You next,' he said, charging fiercely at me. He got closer and closer, almost touching me. I took off the 3D glasses and the film returned to normal.

David McNamee
St Columb's College, Derry

The Field And The Closet

Thomas opened the door only to gaze in horror. He slammed it, sweating and scared. He found a small, tight closet and tucked himself in, still panting from the fear he'd seen in the field. His worst fear - open spaces.

Sean McCafferty (12)
St Columb's College, Derry

The Dentist

'Here he comes,' said John. 'He is coming with a tray of weapons. Help!' he shouted. But he was strapped to a chair. 'Please do not do it,' said John. But before he knew it, it was over. 'There you go,' said Mum, 'You're out of the dentist.'

Gavin O'Neill (12)
St Columb's College, Derry

Mashed Potatoes

She lifted her weapon, steadied her aim, with hammer blows, she started to destroy her target. Again and again she struck them. Soon it was over. She lifted her head with a cheerful smile and voice to match, she chimed, 'Who wants mashed potatoes?'

David Lynch (12)
St Columb's College, Derry

One Halloween Night

One Halloween night, James looked out of the window. He heard the cry of a baby. The doorbell rang. As he edged closer to the door, he got very scared. He was too slow. Yes, the trick or treaters had come and taken every sweet in the house.

Slam!

'Bye!'

Matthew Brown (12)
St Columb's College, Derry

The Penalty

Danny Collins was on a run. He easily beat Tom and Michael. He was bearing down on me. I made myself big, but he rounded me. I had to dive in. *No!* Penalty! He was shooting right. What a save! But the ball was still going in. Michael reacted first.

Caolán Gormley (12)
St Columb's College, Derry

Game Over

'Argh!' shouted Rex, he got bitten in the back by a
hungry zombie!
He lay there on the ground, bleeding while
his friend stood by him, shooting the zombie
that killed his companion. He knelt beside Rex
sobbing, 'You could have pressed triangle, square,
square to survive that last level!'

Macky Martin (13)
St Columb's College, Derry

Goal!

As I walked on the pitch, I felt the adrenaline rush through me. I was the centre of attention, standing in the middle of the field. I was running towards the goal, at full pace. My heart was beating like a drum. I made the shot and it catapulted in.

Thomas Deery (12)
St Columb's College, Derry

The School

One day it's all good, you are just plain Jimmy
Harper. You are the class bully. Everybody fears
you.
But one day a new kid comes to school. Everyone
is scared of him, not you! The bully has become
the victim.

Tiarnan Canning
St Columb's College, Derry

Untitled

This teenager was walking down the street, when a madman was driving at a speed of 200mph down the road. He was getting chased by the police and he was knocked over.
Five days later two wee boys found his phone on the road.

Jerome Marshall (11)
St Columb's College, Derry

Banged-Up Pencil

Pencil only used twice, Tommy was a lonely boy. All of the kids ribbed him, because he had this banged-up pencil. He was so fed up, he sharpened it and got revenge on all of the kids who ribbed him. The police couldn't find any traces, just pencil marks.

Vincent Callaghan (12)
St Columb's College, Derry

Ghost!

Andrew was home alone, in bed. It was quiet, except for the dripping in the basement. Suddenly, he heard the window clank. Nothing. But seconds later, the front door flew open and then his bedroom door creaked open. He saw a light shadow. Then it suddenly all went black.

Aodhan Burke (11)
St Columb's College, Derry

City's Name Holds Crockery

'Help me with this puzzle,' said the man to the
boy. 'City's name holds crockery?'
'What about Derry?' said the boy, 'You see, in
Irish, in school, we learned that Derry is Doire,
which means Oakgrove and a dresser can be
made from an oak tree.'
'Well done!' said he.

Darragh MacFarland (12)
St Columb's College, Derry

One More Kill!

I was on the battlefield, pushing against the
enemy, another kill and I got made up to captain.
I was lining up my shot, ready to pull the trigger.
Bang! A grenade hit me. I set down the controller
and said, 'That's the last time I play 'Call of Duty'.

Conal McFeely (11)
St Columb's College, Derry

Untitled

Knowing this day would come, I'd prepared for ages. I still felt queasy on the day. Futures could be decided on it alone. In its own right, this was judgement day for some. Even the strongest crack under the pressure. The moment had come. I sat to take the test.

Conor O'Connell (13)
St Columb's College, Derry

That Creature

I've spent two hours hunting that creature. Two hours of hell. I need a break, but I can't stop now. I'm so close now, I can taste it. As dusk approaches, I catch a glimpse of it, hiding in a corner. I grab it, laughing, shouting, 'Found you, son!'

Shaun McDermott (14)
St Columb's College, Derry

Hot Pursuit

I rushed to the car. As I sped away, I knew I had to get there in time, but as I got near, police lights appeared behind. But I had to get there in time, so I sped round the corner and said, 'One Big Mac please ...'

Caolan Bradley (13)
St Columb's College, Derry

On The Run

He had five minutes. He sped up, checking if the police were after him. They weren't, but roadworks were next. It was the only route. A ramp! He took it. He landed safely. He arrived with a minute left. A man opened the door saying, 'Ah, my pizza, thanks!'

Reuben Hollywood (14)
St Columb's College, Derry

Excessive Speeds

I was flying down the road and all I could see was a blur, I was going that fast! I saw some people walking in the distance. When I went past them, they were shouting, 'Slow down!' Then I heard a click and I noticed my chain had fallen off!

Bradley Coyle (14)
St Columb's College, Derry

The End At The Bus Stop

As the bus came towards him, he was relieved after rushing the morning ritual, and sprinting down the street. But as the bus came hurtling towards him, relief turned into panic! No! Is this the end? It was indeed the end of his social life. He'd forgotten his English project.

Caolán Duffy (13)
St Columb's College, Derry

Humpty Dumpty - A Horse's View

They rode me to the scene. There was shell everywhere. They parked me beside him. I stared at the wall, thinking about my wages. I looked over the wall and saw the yellow brick road. I fell asleep just as they finished. I fell on him and he broke again!

Conor McConnellogue (13)
St Columb's College, Derry

The 'Almost' Successful Escape

Rob couldn't breathe. Smoke covered the
building, which made it difficult to see past the
burning flames. Rob didn't think he was a goner,
he knew he was a goner! Before he descended,
he could see a fireman in the distance, but it was
too late ... Rob had departed.

Christopher O'Neill (12)
St Columb's College, Derry

Dave

Dave stared into my eyes. There was blood gushing from his chest. This is what I'd been most terrified of since the start of this campaign. My best friend was dying. I stood up in anger and fired my semi-automatic rifle randomly at the enemy.
Then, I killed myself.

Rossa O'Dochartaigh (13)
St Columb's College, Derry

Deserted

Sean is walking through the desert, scorched, burnt, toasted. He needs food and water, but all he sees is desert creatures. He is tempted. He has to. *Crunch!* The boy has eaten. It didn't go down well, but he is no longer hungry. He must now have water to survive …

Kristian Harley (13)
St Columb's College, Derry

The Boy Who Tapped

There was a boy who went through a graveyard and he kept turning around, because he thought somebody tapped him on the head. He ran home and cried.
The next day his friends thought he was crazy. He never tapped again and so the tapping had never came back.

Frank Callaghan (13)
St Columb's College, Derry

Close Call

A man broke into my house and held me up with a gun. I just about phoned the police. Then he went around my house stealing everything. He was ready to go, so he was going to shoot me. *Bang!* The police shot him!

Cahir Campbell (13)
St Columb's College, Derry

The Shot

Bob readied himself for the shot, aiming down the sights of the metal frame. It was his last round. One shot left. Holding his breath, hands trembling, he pushed. The ball travelled at speed and hit its mark. *Strike!* A perfect game of bowling!

Anthony McGuigan
St Columb's College, Derry

War

I was running up the battlefield facing the enemies. Fear was in their eyes. I was one on one with the opposition. Terror was in their souls, but only rage in my eyes.
Next thing, keeper attacked. We were defeated.

Gavin Doherty (13)
St Columb's College, Derry

The Hunter

The hunter was just about to turn the trigger on an innocent lion. He heard a rustle in the dried-up weeds from behind. He was turning round and he only got a glance of a lion's paws as it punched on him.

Michael Lynch (12)
St Columb's College, Derry

The Mystery Man

Every day he comes and we try to catch him, but we never do. I hate him with those big eyes, his wide grin and his stupid pale face. Ah, he went right by me. Where did he go? I think he's away. Ah, well, we will get Pacman someday.

Odhran Doherty (13)
St Columb's College, Derry

3,000 AD

Jamie was sitting, waiting for the next attack. His rocket had been flying around space, waiting. All was quiet, when suddenly a huge meteor shower was coming his way. He twisted and turned, trying to dodge out of the way, then started shooting missiles and then …
'Dinner, Jamie!' Mum called.

David Hughes (12)
St Columb's College, Derry

The Frantic Chase

The huge black figure swooped down upon me. Its claws missed me by inches. I ran through the alley, hoping to escape this monster, which was gaining on me. I saw a gap in the wall and dived in. I heard the crow crash and laughed, while I nibbled cheese.

Emmett Harkin (12)
St Columb's College, Derry

Kangaroo Bite

One day a man went out to a forest. He took with him his gun. He shot at something. It was a kangaroo. The kangaroo hopped up at him, kicked him in the stomach and bit his nose.

Malachy Campbell (12)
St Columb's College, Derry

The Shadow In The Dark

A dark shadow crept along the wall in the distance. I could hear the sound of boots thudding in collision with the ground. I could see a vague figure stride towards me in the moonlight and it spoke …

'You forgot your coat, dear.' It was my mum.

Dermot McCarron (12)
St Columb's College, Derry

The Nursery

Roaring, kicking and running mad. Noise from room to room. Guards tormented, waiting for their shifts to end. Sometimes the guards and prisoners just about make it out. Some say their strategies of hiding stash are quick and simple. Welcome to nursery.

Timothy Cullen (13)
St Columb's College, Derry

The Creature!

I was lying on my bed, when a crackling noise sounded outside my door. I opened my door so I could peer out to the hall. There was a large, hairy beast eating my mother! My dad was decapitated. My door creaked, the beast turned and ran at me. *Argh!*

Peter Sheerin (13)
St Columb's College, Derry

Say Your Prayers!

He walked in with a chainsaw in hand. He roared, 'Say your prayers!' He slowly walked towards the bartender and kicked him hard in the centre of his spine. He sawed his legs off and put them in a bag. Then disappeared. The police finally tracked him down, 'You're nicked!'

Emmet Brown (13)
St Columb's College, Derry

It Was A Lucky Escape

Me and my friend came through a dark alley, as a car came speeding at us with no lights on. The car kept coming at us then he started shooting at us. I made a run for the big wall. I got over. It was a lucky escape for me!

Ryan Jones (13)
St Columb's College, Derry

Wrong Man Caught Out

David got bullied in school because he was fat.
David was very sensitive and was very upset
about being bullied. David was bullied for many
months. Boys were teasing him again. There was
glue on David's chair, he didn't realise and sat
down. Teacher walked in, I'd just hit Jimmy!

Connor Harkin (12)
St Columb's College, Derry

The Ghostly Mansion

Charlie crept up to the 'haunted' mansion. He didn't want to do this dare, but he wasn't letting Louie have the satisfaction of calling him chicken. He opened the door. 'Hello?' he called. No answer. He crept into the hall. He went further in. Slowly, the door closed and locked.

David Trotter (14)
St Columb's College, Derry

War!

I am running faster! Bullets flying by. I see my
friend, John, but he is hurt, so I run to him. *Bang!*
A massive explosion. I am injured. A Japanese
soldier comes over. I look down his gun. He
shoots me.
I turn off the Xbox.

Cathal O'Reilly (13)
St Columb's College, Derry

'Nam

I was on the helicopter on my way to South Vietnam. I didn't realise what I'd signed up for. Vietcong were everywhere. Bullets whizzing past my head, so I had to remember my captain's advice. 'Whatever you do, don't hold an unpinned grenade too long!'
Unfortunately, I hadn't listened.

Mark Stewart (14)

St Columb's College, Derry

Blood Drops

'Oh no!' said Ben, 'It's blood.' Ben wondered where this blood could have come from. He remembered that his dog had been really quiet. He ran as fast as humanly possible. *'Phew!'* he said, as he felt more calm. Then he saw his dog beside a dead rat.

Niall Edwards (13)
St Columb's College, Derry

Oh No! The Police!

The police pull up at my house. They get out of a SWAT vehicle. They get guns. They run up to my door and bust it through. They say, 'Give us the drugs!' They see me and walk away. I smile and say, 'Phew!'

Rhys Browne (13)
St Columb's College, Derry

The Explosion

Bang! There was an explosion. I was injured, I felt
a severe pain. Next thing I remember is waking
up in hospital, the pain is getting worse. *'Ouch!'*
I shout. The doctor comes running in. 'What's
wrong with my leg?'
The doctor says, 'Sorry, we had to amputate.'

Lee McGuinness (13)
St Columb's College, Derry

Sudden Death

It's just me and the keeper now. If I score this penalty we win the World Cup. If I miss, then it is in their hands. One last look at the keeper and I hit it as hard as I can in the direction of the goal. *Yes!* We've won!

Niall Doherty (14)
St Columb's College, Derry

Boom!

I go to the shop to get some spuds for my mum. When I arrive there are police outside. *Boom!* A huge explosion, people screaming and shouting, 'A bomb!' The medics rush to the rescue of the injured, but for some it is too late!

Keelan Maguire (13)
St Columb's College, Derry

Leaping

I looked into its eyes. It held my gaze. I knew
it would make its move. It leapt upon me and
knocked me over. I closed my eyes tight. It licked
me and barked. I pushed Sparky off me and
laughed. Sparky jumped and joined in with a howl.

Oran Campbell (12)
St Columb's College, Derry

Dark Valley

As I walk down a scary lane, I hear footsteps.
I turn around to see a man in a dark coat with
a hat, looking at me in a scary way. He starts
running towards me, so I run as fast as I can. A
sigh of relief … he's gone.

Eoin McNeill (12)
St Columb's College, Derry

Normal Activity

I was awoken by a loud bark. It sounded quite like a contained scream. I looked at my clock, midnight sharp! My curtains were blowing. Moonlight shone through my open window. I checked outside. It was clear the bark had come from a dog. So I went back to sleep.

Ryan Magee (12)
St Columb's College, Derry

The Game

There was a man who was playing a baseball game and the other team was throwing against him. He was the best batsman and he had to get a home run, but suddenly, something hit him. It was small and hard. He was hurt. What was it that hit him?

Niall Boyle (12)
St Columb's College, Derry

A Tense Game

I looked into his eyes and saw desire. I knew what he wanted and I thought he was going to get it. I looked down again and my heart missed a beat. I grabbed my piece and moved it. 'Checkmate,' I said, overjoyed with victory.

Seán Curran (13)
St Columb's College, Derry

Mystery In The Deep

In pitch darkness, we set the boat up at the jetty
and sailed out to sea. We waited for hours. *Bang!*
We all jumped. I grabbed my fishing rod and
struggled to reel the fish in. *Snap* went my rod, as
it followed my fish away.

Dylan Carr (12)
St Columb's College, Derry

The Sniper

He loads the bolt. Everything must be silent and steady. The sight is dusty, with streaks of light flashing across the lens. It is hard to see the target over one kilometre away. He can hear everything now. He goes to take the shot … miss.

Aaron Cassidy (13)
St Columb's College, Derry

Skyline Chairs

The terrifying flying chairs swayed in front of me. Every time they went up, they looked like they were banging on Heaven. The creak of the metal frame screeched through my brain. I was terrified. They went so fast. Dad shouted, 'Jack, come on! I'll push you on the swing!'

Ryan Butler (13)
St Columb's College, Derry

The Hunger

As I walked through the doors, I saw a McDonald's right in front of me. Suddenly I became extremely hungry. My granny came out and started playing football with Bob. I got the money from my mum and ran across to McDonald's. 'Oh no!' It was closed!

Dominic McCow (13)
St Columb's College, Derry

Zombies

I walked into the supermarket. There wasn't anyone there. Suddenly a zombie started sprinting at me. I panicked. I ran, past the bread, then the milk, into the gun section. I lifted the closest gun and shot off the zombie's disgusting and rotting head. Blood splattered over the rotting apples.

Kevin McGill (13)
St Columb's College, Derry

Dorothy

Dorothy lived in a wood.
One day she found a lake. She headed back, planning on coming back, but she had forgotten her way. In her panic, she slipped into the lake to find she was underground. Multicoloured dwarves pressed towards her and pounced on her.
Then she woke up.

Tiarnán McCartney (12)
St Columb's College, Derry

The Man-Eating Dog!

I was running fast, when a vicious, man-eating dog chased me. There was a massive river, so I jumped as high as I could. My foot got stuck between jagged stones. I pulled and tugged at it, but my foot wouldn't move. It came closer and closer, but then ...

Ronan McConnell (12)
St Columb's College, Derry

Wisdom Dies

Samos was an old man, nobody liked him. Samos was a wise man, but because he was old, his time was running out.

One day a boy saw Samos lying on the ground outside his hut. His soul went up and Samos' body was ready to go to Heaven.

Ronan Duddy (12)
St Columb's College, Derry

Full Moon

He was running for his life, through a gruesome,
blood-stricken forest. He tripped and landed on
his face. 'No!' he shouted, battering the damp
forest floor. The full moon was rising quickly. His
body started its transformation. He got more
muscular. He was a wereling on a murderous
path.

Ciaran Ball (12)
St Columb's College, Derry

The Betrayal

'You dare betray the brotherhood!' asked the master. He moved towards Derven. He was on his knees.

'I … didn't mean … to,' whimpered Derven.

'Ah, you've admitted it. You have indeed betrayed us, Derven. You know the vows. You must perish,' said the master. Suddenly he fell, knife in his back.

Colum Ferry (12)
St Columb's College, Derry

Run!

He kept running, as fast as he could. The beast was getting closer. He could see its big eyes when he looked back. The beast was fast. The advantage was that the ground was slippery. It jumped, its shadow covered Melvin. It landed in front of him, its claws ready ...

Dominic Watt (13)
St Columb's College, Derry

Bad Luck

Patrick bought a dog. He was nice and big.
Two days later, Patrick saw his dog was very sick.
Patrick was sad. He went to the vet with his dog
and the doctor said he was very sick. He went
home.
Then a few minutes later, his lovely dog died.

Lakas Myszak (13)
St Columb's College, Derry

Assassination

In the sixties an assassin called Johannes was hired to kill someone. The only thing was, he wasn't told what he looked like or what his name was. He only knew where to find him. So that night he set up his sniper on the roof and shot … his father.

Aaron Craig (12)
St Columb's College, Derry

Room 911

There was a family called Jacobs. They were planning to go to a hotel, while their house was renovated. The hotel was called Hotel Schloss. It was situated in a desolate area and was pretty rundown. When they arrived at the hotel, they had no idea what was coming next.

Shane Carlin (12)
St Columb's College, Derry

Nicked!

'Listen up, team! The next case is a big one! This guy is Mister Big! Big Nick is wanted all across the northern hemisphere, shipping goods illegally across borders, working children in sweat shops, not to mention animal cruelty! You may know him as Santa Claus!'

Aidan McCollum (13)
St Columb's College, Derry

Untitled

He stumbled recklessly through the overgrown forest. Trembling at the crack of the bark below his sodden shoes, they were on his case … As the gun fired, a great sound erupted into the clear night. It pierced through the air like lightning into his heart, killing him on the spot.

Patrick Deboys (16)
Slemish College, Ballymena

Untitled

Silence surrounds the room. Tense, tortured,
troubled, the vulnerable victims wait in the
dark, eerie room. The atmosphere is cold, like
the heart of a murderer. Their fate is near. The
footsteps are getting creepier, clearer … closer.
Mrs Honey strolls viciously in with the hated
exams for terrified teenagers.

Lauren Gault (16)

Slemish College, Ballymena

The Darkness

The hairs on the back of my neck stood on end.
What could I do? I stepped forward, but he pulled
me back. 'Don't leave,' he whispered. I turned
around and looked him in the eye.
'I'll be back tomorrow,' I whispered and I left him
in the darkness, alone.

Rebecca Magill (13)
Slemish College, Ballymena

Royal Blue

The box swings frantically agape. 'And they're off!'
The clip-clop of the galloping horses rings in the
increasingly anxious minds of the eager fans as
the race continues. The horse in royal blue suede,
reins above the rest. As the final straight nears,
there is only one clear winner.

Sean Fox & Cillein McGlade (16)
Slemish College, Ballymena

Information

We hope you have enjoyed reading this book - and that you will continue to enjoy it in the coming years.

If you like reading and writing, drop us a line or give us a call and we'll send you a free information pack. Alternatively visit our website at **www.youngwriters.co.uk**

Write to:

Young Writers Information,
Remus House,
Coltsfoot Drive,
Peterborough,
PE2 9JX

Tel: (01733) 890066
Email: youngwriters@forwardpress.co.uk